WARNING!!!!

THIS BOOK IS FOR AUNTS AND UNCLES,
NIECES AND NEPHEWS ONLY!

(THE SECRET PASSWORD IS *CAPEESH* . . . CAPEESH?)

Signed, THE SECRET SOCIETY OF AUNTS & UNCLES

For Mona and Gigi—Love, Uncle Jake
—J.G.

For Nancy, who sees me
—G.C.

For Anya and Jayda
—D.S.

A Feiwel and Friends Book • An imprint of Macmillan Publishing Group, LLC • 120 Broadway, New York, NY 10271
mackids.com

Our books may be purchased in bulk for promotional, educational, or business use.
Please contact your local bookseller or the Macmillan Corporate and Premium Sales Department
at (800) 221-7945 ext. 5442 or by email at MacmillanSpecialMarkets@macmillan.com.

Library of Congress Cataloging-in-Publication Data is available

First edition, 2023
Book design by Rich Deas and Kathleen Breitenfeld • Feiwel and Friends logo designed by Filomena Tuosto
Printed in China by R.R. Donnelly; Asia Printing Solutions Ltd., Dongguan City, Guangdong Province

978-1-250-77699-0 (hardcover)
1 3 5 7 9 10 8 6 4 2

WRITTEN BY: JAKE GYLLENHAAL AND ILLUSTRATIONS

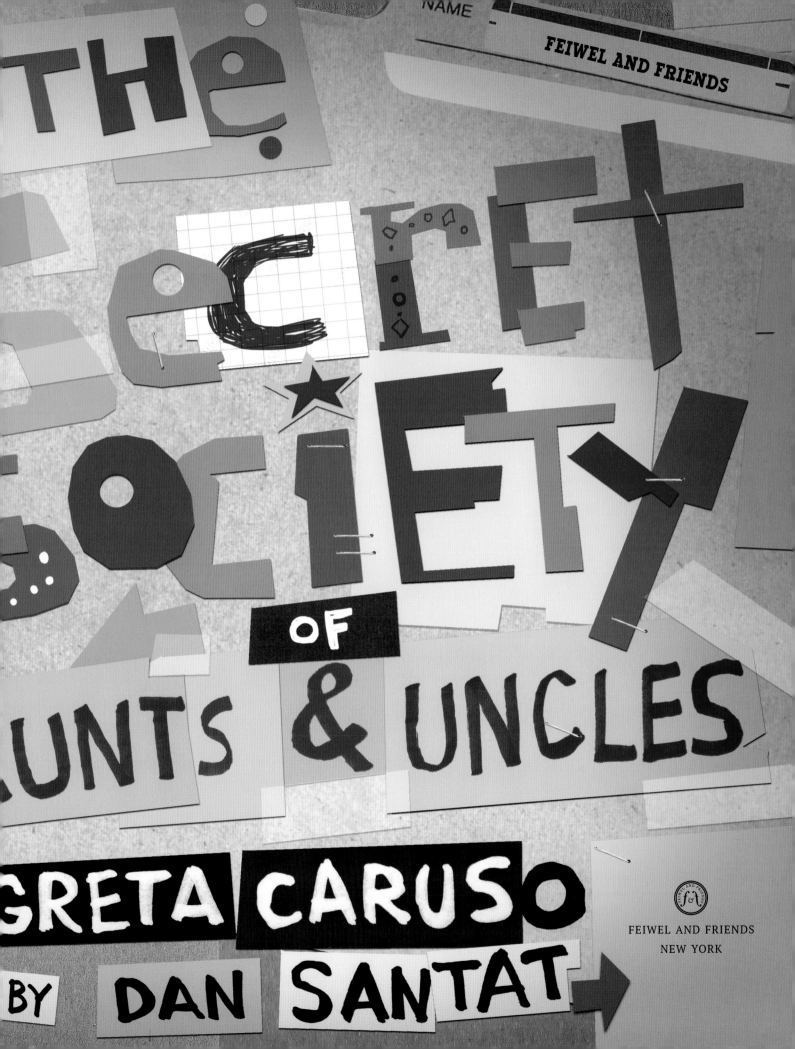

THE SECRET SOCIETY OF AUNTS & UNCLES

GRETA CARUSO

BY DAN SANTAT

FEIWEL AND FRIENDS

FEIWEL AND FRIENDS
NEW YORK

Leo was a shy boy.

He loved to dance . . .

. . . but his glasses always got in the way.

Just when things couldn't get any worse . . .

"Oh no, Uncle Mo!"

"Hello, Leonard, I'm in town for a rubber band convention. Your mom asked me to babysit tonight."

Rubber band convention? That's so boring! thought Leo.

"Rules for the car: No drinking. The leather is sensitive to liquids. And please, no gum—especially if it's bubble. No bubbles. Bubbles are sticky icky icky! Bedtime is at 8 P.M. And no dessert tonight. Your mom said."

"You have rules for everything!"

Leo couldn't help but think:

YOU ARE THE WORST UNC...

"Out of the car and follow us!" rang a voice from the darkness.

"I am the Great-Aunt Gloria,
and this handsome fellow is
Uncle Munkle Carbunkle!" bellowed an extremely
tall woman standing next to a very small man.

"Welcome to the wonderful in-between,
where no parent ever steps toe,
much less foot, or hoof, or paw."

THE SECRET SOCIETY OF AU

"Here we preserve the ancient arts of Auntieology and Uncleology. Something you clearly know NOTHING about, so you shall be tested by our distinguished panel of nephews and nieces."

ROOM 007

"What time is bedtime?" a niece shouted from the stands.
"Eight o'clock?" guessed a confused Mo.

All the kids shook their heads.

"Bedtime is always three minutes before Mom and Dad get home!" shouted Uncle Munkle Carbunkle in disappointment.

"Next lesson!"

Great-Aunt Gloria pointed at Mo. "What should he eat first: broccoli or a brownie sundae with ice cream and hot fudge?"

"Vegetables, of course!"

Leo hid his face.

"Dinner and dessert go in and outta the same place! Capeesh?! What difference does it make which one you eat first?!"

"Oh no, Mo! Off to the Un-Uncle Zone," Uncle Munkle Carbunkle said.

"There's only one way out of the Un-Uncle Zone, broccoli breath!" cried Great-Aunt Gloria. "Answer this simple question: What is your nephew's favorite thing to do?!"

Mo blinked. He had no idea.

How could he not know?

CRASH!

So Leo took a deep breath and then decided to . . .

show him.

YIKES-A-RONI! Leo's glasses flew right off!
He tore down the curtain with his arm mid-twirl,

tripped over Mo's foot at the beginning of a long sashay,

and his glasses landed right on Great-Aunt Gloria's head.

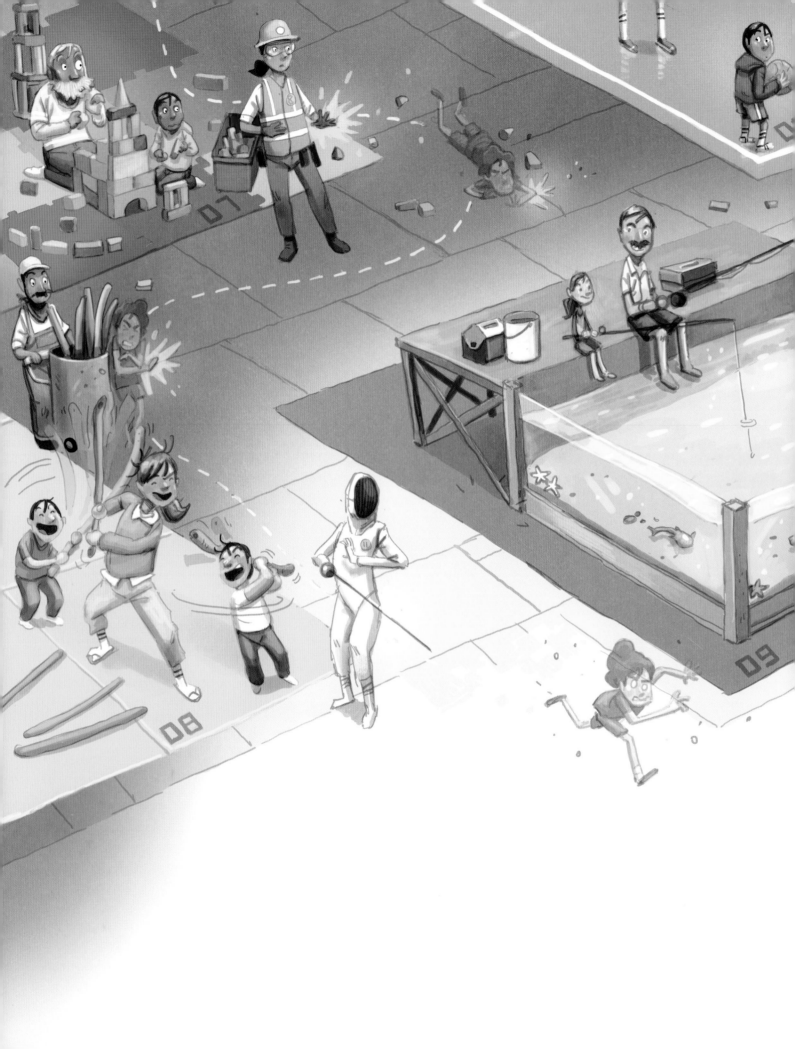

Leo was mortified.

Uncle Mo found Leo sitting alone.

"I'm sorry," Mo said.

"Sorry? You're not even trying."

"I might not have a whole lot to offer,
but would you let me try to help?
I have an idea."

Mo took a rubber band out of his pocket and tied Leo's glasses together.

"I used to wear glasses when I was a kid. Give 'em a spin, now."

A leap!

A flip!

Everyone cheered for Leo's stellar dancing!
"It's the small things that change everything!" Great-Aunt Gloria winked.

GROOMING

NUTRITION

Mo and Leo flew through the rest of Emergency Basic Training.

CRAFTS

TRUST

COOKING

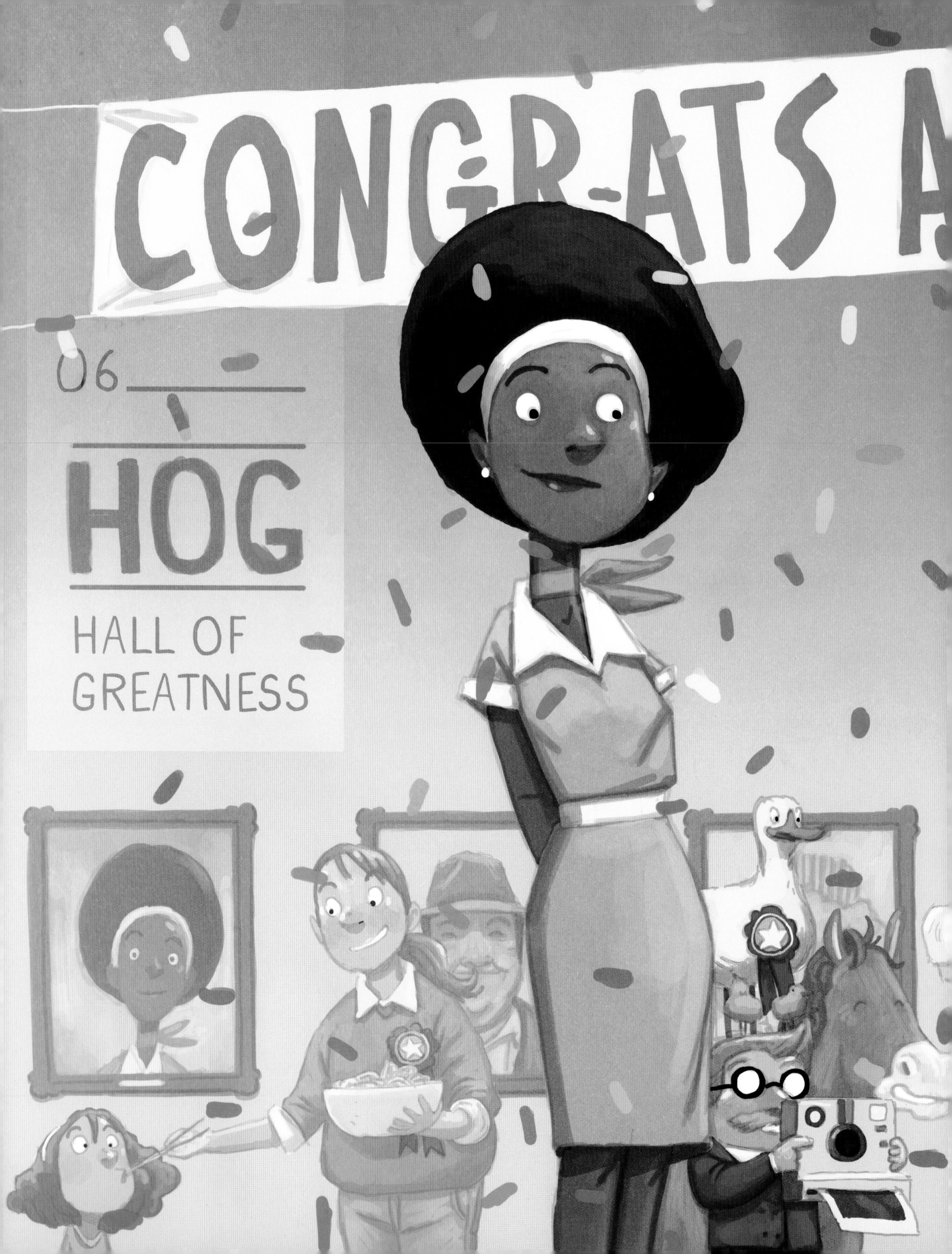
CONGRATS A
06
HOG
HALL OF
GREATNESS

"Congrats, you're officially a beginner uncle! We were worried there for a second! Be sure to come back for some advanced courses!" Great-Aunt Gloria added.

"COME BACK?" asked Leo. "How do we even get he—"

Three minutes before Leo's mom got home, Mo tucked Leo into bed.

"Uncle Mo? I can't see you so well without my glasses."

Mo leaned in. "See me now?"

"Yes. I see you." Leo smiled.

Uncle Mo smiled back.

"And now I see you, too."

Me and Uncle Mo